SOFIA MARTINEZ

Abuela's Special Letters

by Jacqueline Jules

illustrated by Kim Smith

PICTURE WINDOW BOOKS
a capstone imprint

Sofia Martinez is published by
Picture Window Books, a Capstone imprint
1710 Roe Crest Drive
North Mankato, MN 56003
www.mycapstone.com

Library of Congress Cataloging-in-Publication data
is available on the Library of Congress website.

ISBN: 978-1-5158-0728-5 (library binding)
ISBN: 978-1-5158-0732-2 (eBook PDF)

Summary: Sofia is on a mission to make a family
time capsule. The whole family contributes pictures
and special items. Abuela even writes a letter to each
of her grandchildren to be opened in ten years. Can
Sofia really wait fifteen years to find out what that
letter says?

Designer: Aruna Rangarajan
Art Director: Kay Fraser

Printed and bound in China.
9981S17

TABLE OF CONTENTS

CHAPTER 1

The Collection

"¡Atención!" Sofia said. "I need each of you to fill out my question sheet, por favor."

"I can't," Manuel said. "I don't know how to write."

"I'll write for you," Sofia said. "What do you want to be when you grow up?"

"A firefighter," Manuel said.

"Describe yourself in one word," Sofia said.

"Brave!" Manuel said.

Sofia asked more questions. She wrote down Manuel's answers. Then she collected all of the sheets and put them in a cookie tin.

"Why are you putting those papers in a cookie tin?" Manuel asked.

"Because we're making a family time capsule," Sofia said.

"¿Por qué?" Manuel asked.

"So we can have fun in the future by looking at our past," Sofia said.

Sofia's cousins helped her find other things for the time capsule.

"Here's a seashell to remember our beach trips," Alonzo said.

"Here are my favorite drum sticks," Hector said.

"Are you sure?" Sofia asked. "They will stay in the time capsule for ten years."

"Don't worry. I have another pair," Hector said.

"You can take my toy fire truck," Manuel said.

"¡Excelente!" Sofia said.

Except there was a problem.

The cookie tin wouldn't close.

"You need something bigger,"

Alonzo said.

Sofia searched until she found a giant jar of pretzels.

"It's half full," Hector said.

"Sí." Sofia smiled. "Let's start eating!"

CHAPTER 2

Abuela's Addition

Sofia's sisters added Abuela's arroz con leche recipe and Mamá's piano music to the collection.

Then they helped Sofia decorate the jar. They used ribbons and paint. They even put some glitter in the bottom of the container.

"Muy bonito," Elena said.

Later that day, Sofia's family
met in the living room again.

The cousins shared what they
had written for the time capsule.

"I wrote about my dream to be an animal doctor," Luisa said. "You know how I love animals."

"I wrote about my dream to be a drummer in a famous band," Hector said as he drummed a beat on the floor.

"I want to be a superhero," Alonzo said running around, pretending to fly.

"And I want to be a TV reporter," Sofia said. "It's the perfect job for me."

"How did you describe

yourselves?" Papá asked.

Alonzo opened his arms.

"Loud!"

Everyone laughed, especially Tía Carmen. She was always complaining about her loud household.

"Curious,'" Sofia answered.

"¡Me gusta!" Abuela said. "That's exactly what my Sofia is."

Next, Papá held up family pictures. He had some of the house too.

Mamá had a bag of dried marigolds. "Because I love my garden," she said.

Abuela raised a handful of colorful envelopes. "I have a letter for each one of my grandchildren."

"Qué bien," Mamá said. "A special message to read in the future."

"About what?" Sofia asked.

"The person you'll be when you're all grown up," Abuela answered.

"Let me see," Sofia begged.

"No peeking!" Abuela winked.

CHAPTER 3

Too Curious

Sofia sealed the time capsule with strong tape and a sign that said, "TOP SECRET!"

The whole family followed her to a closet under the basement stairs. Papá put the jar on the top shelf. Everyone clapped, except Sofia.

Sofia was thinking about Abuela's special letters. "My abuela knows everything. She must know the future, too," Sofia thought.

That night in bed, Sofia could
not sleep.

"Will I be on TV? Will Luisa
be an animal doctor? What about
Hector? How can I wait ten years
to know?" Sofia wondered aloud.

Sofia crept down to the

basement in her nightgown. The

capsule was way up high. She

would have to climb to reach it.

That turned out to be very
noisy. Boxes dropped from lower
shelves.

Mamá and Papá ran downstairs
to find a mess.

"Lo siento," Sofia said. "I couldn't wait for the future."

"But that's what a time capsule is for," Papá said.

"Yo sé," Sofia said, nodding.

"Why can't you wait?" Mamá asked.

"Abuela's letter," Sofia said. "She knows what I'll be when I grow up."

"I do too." Mamá smiled.

"You do?" Sofia asked.

"Sí," Mamá said. "You'll be

curious!"

"Just like you are now,"

Papá added.

Spanish Glossary

abuela — grandmother

arroz con leche — rice pudding

atención — attention

excelente — great

lo siento — I'm sorry

mamá — mom

me gusta — I like it

muy bonito — very pretty

papá — dad

por favor — please

por qué — why

qué bien — how nice

sí — yes

tía — aunt

yo sé — I know

Talk It Out

1. Time capsules capture a moment in the past. Why is the past important?

2. What do you think you would find in a time capsule from one hundred years ago?

3. Were you surprised that Sofia tried to look in the capsule early? Why or why not?

Write It Down

1. Write a paragraph about what you want to be when you grow up.

2. Write a letter about one of your friends to put in a time capsule. Describe what you think he/she will do in the future.

3. Write a paragraph about three items you would add to a time capsule.

About the Author

Jacqueline Jules is the award-winning author of thirty children's books, including *No English* (2012 Forward National Literature Award), *Zapato Power: Freddie Ramos Takes Off* (2010 CYBILS Literary Award, Maryland Blue Crab Young Reader Honor Award, and ALSC Great Early Elementary Reads), and *Freddie Ramos Makes a Splash* (named on 2013 List of Best Children's Books of the Year by Bank Street College Committee).

When not reading, writing, or teaching, Jacqueline enjoys time with her family in northern Virginia.

About the Illustrator

Kim Smith has worked in magazines, advertising, animation, and children's gaming. She studied illustration at the Alberta College of Art and Design in Calgary, Alberta, where she now resides.

Kim is the illustrator of the middle-grade mystery series *The Ghost and Max Monroe*, the picture book *Over the River and Through the Woods*, and the cover of the middle-grade novel *How to Make a Million*.

FUN
doesn't stop here!

- Videos & Contests
- Games & Puzzles
- Friends & Favorites
- Authors & Illustrators

Discover more at
www.capstonekids.com

See you soon!
¡Nos Vemos pronto!